Joe Potato's Real Life Recipes

Tall Tales and Short Stories

By Meriwether O'Connor

Appalachia North

Published by Appalachia North
PO Box 57, East Dixfield, Maine 04227 USA

ISBN: 9780692278093

"Joe Potato" & "Malachi Jones" first appeared in *Dew on the Kudzu.*

"The Troll Of Mustard Creek Bridge", "Two Sides To Every Story", and "Matilda Gets A Chicken" first appeared in *Fiction365.*

"Eating Crow" first appeared in *Graze.*

For a behind-the-scenes look at *The Squirrel,* check out sketchbookproject.com or the Brooklyn Art Library

Cover photo by Jack Delano, Library of Congress, Prints & Photographs Division, FSA-OWI Collection, LC-DIG-ppmsc-00255

For SD, MG and DG,
I always thought you were lying
when you said I could do it.
Thanks for believing
long before I ever could.

For JFK, who surprised me by her kindness.

And for DM and DM,
thanks for taking a chance!

Acknowledgements

This book has been a long time in the making. Many thanks to the foundations who helped along the way, including Hedgebrook, who first took a chance on me, and Mesa Refuge, Blue Mountain Lake and Colorado Art Ranch. Thanks also to Astraea, whose grant fifteen years ago literally changed my life!

Table of Contents

Table of Contents

The Squirrel

The squirrel ate a small hole in the wall. It didn't have to be large, as it was not a raccoon or a dog or even a burglar. But, a squirrel. Who only wanted nuts or cardboard or peanut butter. Or, perhaps worse, to chew through brand new wiring. Or, far worse, through older wiring that didn't need any help catching fire. It could do that all by itself, thank you very much.

This was the tiny hole, but still too large for a mouse, that Gardenia found one morning as she got up too early even for the crows. It was Saturday, and sane folk were still in bed under the covers, and brave ones had not yet gotten home from gallivanting around.

Being neither brave nor fancy, Gardenia was at home where she belonged, eyeing a hole just above the baseboard in her home. The wall was part metal so how a squirrel chewed through was difficult to discern. She had added wood outside to shelter from the wind. Perhaps the wood had been tasty, the old metal wall of the trailer had a crack at the seam and, well, there you go.

She had heard birds chirping far too early that morning. Until she walked into the kitchen, she had not realized that her over-loud birds were instead an ambitious squirrel in the next room. Nothing should chirp so early in the morning. Or, if it couldn't make an appointment, perhaps at least wait til 9am when the cow had been brought round and the wood collected and clothes steamed and even perhaps a few eggs brought to neighbors.

She sat down with her coffee, no cream, and waited. Her left foot kicked the rung of the chair as ideas flipped through her awfully red curls. Too red, she'd been told. If they'd come out of a box, she'd have been able to adjust down a notch to just slightly red. Or, a tiny tint above average. But, these were her curls and God (though perhaps goaded by the townspeople) had never yet adjusted them any way but up.

As she got older, the fire grew stronger. She kept it cut short, hoping in some manner to slow the spread of color but it seemed instead like pruning roses. Each time she sliced through the red curls they grew back stronger and more fierce.

Just last Sunday in church the woman behind her had complained she couldn't hear the sermon due to the loud humming of Gardenia's hair. The hair loved to be in church and would almost applaud, if you could call it that, with the tips, as Gardenia swung with the music, eyes closed.

Today, the hair was up in a kerchief the way the old ladies wore theirs. She didn't knot it, but put another band of material over it to sort of make a turban, if you will. She was queen of the home, if nowhere else, and a turban she could wear. At least on a Saturday morning.

The squirrel heard Gardenia's tapping and misunderstood. He thought perhaps a woodpecker was searching for worms and leaving stray nuts falling around his industry by accident. He sniffed from afar.

Gardenia's flip flop had about flopped out. The rubber should have died ages ago, but since it was not alive, it kept trotting on, oblivious to the discomfort of being torn in two a day at a time. Her toes were strong, like thumbs. She could grasp things with them, and did. Both to the amusement or horror, depending, of whoever watched. She had learned not to drink with them or pick up food, but she would pick up things off the ground and toss it up into her palm to stick in her coat pocket. It saved bending over, and what was wrong with that?

Her thumb toes were busy tapping the chair, and the squirrel sat nearby. Sniffing. At a bit before seven, he made his move. He ran along the baseboard under the table and looked for the peanut butter ball that had been dropped behind the cabinets after the wake for the neighbor last Sunday. A peanut with no shell to crack was a treat for any squirrel, especially one living in a home, even if temporarily, that had not seen its share of treats in the world.

Gardenia thought she saw a scurry but then she thought she saw a lot of things. Her eyes were tired and often she would close them, peacefully, as if it were raining. Her thumb toes tapped on and the squirrel kept in pursuit of the peanut ball which had rolled forward as he'd overestimated and jumped with too much force, even for a squirrel.

The squirrel finished up the last crumbs and paused. The thumb toes were a nice patter in his day, like rain, only not wet. No need to run as the red lady's eyes were closed and at peace. The squirrel was thirsty, but there was no leaky pipe inside for him to drink from. Gardenia's coffee was too high on the table, guarded by her true thumbs, even if it hadn't been boilt to Jesus and too hot to drink. He'd tried some before at night and had not been left satisfied.

Now, we are all of us under the sun, meat. Gardenia included and she knew it. One of the few humans who did, actually. The few others that realized it, turned a hard heart to animals, pushing away the knowledge of their own demise. Those who didn't know or believe they were meat were not worse. But. Not better.

Gardenia's eyes were closed but she heard the patter of her dinner. It was small, but there. She didn't know the squirrel's name or family or whereabouts, but his pattering in her home without first knocking at the front door had definitely put him into the dinner category.

Now, she had eaten many things in life but not squirrel. Some much bigger, a few, out of necessity, smaller. Her stomach didn't care to remember those the cat had been fond of sharing during the cold winters, and who was she to turn down a handsome tom whom she has put so much milk and cream towards during the good times of the past?

The squirrel was now on her radar the way a sale on pantsuits or high-heeled shoes might be for a city woman. She was curious, and she was hungry, the basic beginning of any predator. The squirrel shifted his hind legs as she stopped tapping with her thumb toe.

They say human sweat changes with fear. It's also possible that something changes in the eye with hunger. Though they were closed, perhaps there was an odd wrinkle under the right one, or maybe her left forefinger scratched her in a very unfortunate away. Regardless, the squirrel moved a centimeter to the left to be under the lip of the white stove.

Gardenia opened an eye. She saw nothing. She closed it and sat. She tapped. She opened another. More tapping.

The squirrel began eyeing his handiwork on the wall and began, perhaps, wishing he'd busted into someone else's home. Perhaps someone with better crumbs and a much fuller belly. Someone whom age had weakened not strengthened. Not someone like Gardenia.

She considered the .22 by the door. Outside, that would suffice. Inside, it might break her china with rose patterns on the teacups. Eating today was worth a lot, but not that. Though, of course, she had coffee, she would not deny that. And it did kill the hunger as they said.

She didn't smoke, though, didn't cotton to that at all. Not even chaw. Those took away hunger only second to food itself. Maybe even better, for some.

But back to the squirrel. Its tail which made no noise at all, caught a dust angel under the stove. Gardenia heard nothing. But. She moved one foot forward, it was so instinctual it didn't matter which one.

A predatory dance had begun which would end with a squirrel in the pot, a broken teacup or a woman begging dried corn for chicken feed off the neighbors then boiling it up like Jesus in the same pot in place of the squirrel. He had definitely come into the wrong home.

Gardenia lunged and grabbed at nothing but nothing is sometimes a squirrel tail musty with dust. It lunged for her face in the way only something getting out, up and over anything in its way can. She screamed out of fear, as anything coming straight at you is terrifying even if will be your dinner in a moment. Only because there is a God (though you might disagree on several counts) her hand again caught the squirrel, this time by a little paw. She held on and her heart sunk.

Even though death was ringing in her ears, breaking its leg beforehand was not on even her most desperate agenda. Her mother had once followed a deer three days after a poor shot to end its misery for good. To see the woman's clothes as torn as what would eventually happen to the deer left an impression that could not be forgotten by the tinkering of a squirrel in her kitchen. Both the necessity of death and the avoidance of pain were hers by blood right, which you will find honest or ridiculous or even perhaps cruel depending on your own birthright.

Though the leg didn't snap, she vomited as if it had. She shoved the squirrel into the pocket of her house dress then pressed a dishtowel over it, running and frothing and running and frothing til she found an old metal coffee can to put it in. She had taken game from a distance and farm animals from quite close up. But this was confusing. The cat would know what to do, but it had not even been woken up by the scuffle, still full from two days ago finding snakes in the yard and the last of her cream she had frozen for it from last fall. When it was fat like that you couldn't get it to wash its face much less take care of a squirrel.

This may have been better or worse for the squirrel. Death is death. When Gardenia died, if she died at home, the cat might take her toes a few at a time til a neighbor passed by not having seen her at the store for a while. If she died in the yard, putting out clothes, a bear or a coyote might come along for a snack. If she died in the hospital, white masked people would formaldehyde her out of existence so that no creature would or could recognize her as having once been alive.

The squirrel was alive in the tin. Gardenia was, too, in her tin can home with wood on the outside to decorate it up and warm it up a bit. She reached for her tools and took care of it the way she would a chicken if they had not died last week when the coyotes came down from the hills because of the drought. The eggs in the fridge were better for barter than eating, as the neighbors craved them in a way only people who had never grown their own could.

In a moment, the squirrel was meat. It meant Gardenia would live another three days, maybe more. The cat, at least a week if he kept up the luck he'd had most of his life. The sun would rise. The sun would fall. And that was that. No matter what.

Gardenia's Squirrel with Hot Coffee

Whether you get your own squirrel from the Sears mail order catalogue, off the wall in your well-equipped kitchen, or outside in the woods, prepare it as you would any wild meat. Remember, marinating is your friend in times like this. Beer, wine, salad dressing or Coke all make a good soak. Let sit for an hour to a couple of days in the fridge, your choice. (Your need for supper versus your wish for a tender bite being the deciding factor here.)

Meat you buy in the store is already "aged". All you're doing with fresh meat is letting it rest so it becomes tender as well. Now, if you're already used to fresh meat, then you might just enjoy it the very same day! But, then, you won't need me to tell you that. You already know what you like.

Often, one squirrel will fit easily into a loaf pan. Remember, they are mostly tail! Bake at 350. Or, debone and fry up in a cast iron skillet. Best to fix with starches like rice or potatoes, as you'll get some tasty morsels but not much more off a single squirrel. Nice with a dandelion salad early in the spring.

Add your favorite gravy, and you've got a meal. White gravy with black pepper may be preferred, but some will tell you a brown gravy cannot be beat. Drink with black coffee, as hot as you can stand it.

Gardenia's Thoughts on Black Coffee:

Certainly, you may add cream and sugar to yours, but when you get older, the doctor will just try to convince you to take all the good stuff out, and then where will you be? Always drink it black, and you'll never miss a thing. Or, so my grandmother convinced me. And now I can't stand it any other way. It does grow on you.

Gardenia's Second Thoughts on Squirrel and Black Coffee:

My mom and them always said anything you need you can find in the Sears catalog; it's like Christmas. So, I thought I'd mention it in case you live high up in a city apartment with no squirrels anywhere you look.

The Mail Comes Twice on Mondays

U p in NYC, no...not North Carolina, but the city of New York, Papa hunts apartment rabbits. He sends us notes home in his long, fine handwriting. He doesn't lick the stamps, but presses them on the side of his water glass first to get the damp just right. He says they come out at night, the house rabbits.

He said they are different than ours that live wild outside or lounge in the hay in the barn for just in case. He draws me tiny pictures of them and tells me he leaves snacks out for them at night. He honors them, then eats them. But, he leaves pepperoni and stale bread and even sometimes leftover cheese if he has it. Our rabbits at home, outdoors rabbits, only like vegetables and fruits and rinds of anything and well, of course, grain.

He says city rabbits are hungrier than ours so they will eat meat and even strange things with mold on them that ours would never even bend their noggin to sniff here. He draws me pictures of their whiskers which I like and says he can't quite get their tails exactly as they look in real life, but does his best.

Their tails aren't fluffy, he says, and they are not nice and furry as ours. No fun to pet, he says. No good for winter clothes. So, he sends me pictures he draws but never gloves or hat or what he might have made here. He says he is busy and besides, the colors aren't right. Ours are so much better. Only now he calls them yours. I don't like that.

He tells me they do have birds for eating, not just flying, up there, but your neighbors can't know. He says the birds are so heavy in the sky they break the branches on the tree, and, really, there aren't that many trees, so watch out! They sit on his air conditioner and also outside his window. He says they like sunny days, which there aren't too many of. He says tall buildings are taller than you'd think. He says flying dinner is a real winner when he signs off in a silly mood. He says don't tell your mom. He says see you soon.

One day...I say, I'm going to walk to the station and come see you. I say she won't mind. He says if you show up I'll whip you good. I say you can't catch me, I've gotten faster. He says you ought to go right now and get you a cane off the raspberry bushes in the back for even saying that to me. I laugh, and I do. I really do. I switch the back of the chair with it.

Then I place it in a cup of water, and it fills out the side and falls over, splashing everywhere. I pick it up and try again, this time in an old milk carton, and this time it stays. No fruit on it, just thorns. It will grow or stay still or rot, but it will be here for him to laugh at when he gets back. When he gets back. He will come back.

Papa Daddy's Midnight Dinner for One

How you come by your own personal apartment rabbit is up to you. Myself, I favor a bit of meat and bread, but my neighbor from before swore by peanut butter. Apartment rabbits hate the smell of peppermint, so try not to use that kind of soap on your hands. (I don't think it matters as far as toothpaste.)

If you're "lucky" enough to have a few at once, you can make quite a nice stew. Otherwise, you'll have a decent sandwich, if you can find some pigweed (lamb's quarters) growing down on the block somewhere. I grab some when I come back over the Brooklyn Bridge on Sundays, but that's up to you.

Like barbecue? Try roasting it over the fire on the stove. A skewer works or even a chopstick that you've soaked in water. Or, do it like a marshmallow and just use a stick. If you don't have barbecue sauce, marinate it first in Coke. The sweet helps it taste good and makes for a nice color, too. And, the acid helps break down the meat just like when you used to make fajitas. If you used to make fajitas.

You're on your own as to who you share your recipes with. That's your own business. But if you come up with any nice ones, let me know. And, tell me if there's still pepperweed growing by the plantain across from that pile of bricks where that lady started that garden that never really went anywhere. You know, the one with those almost-potatoes. I miss that pepperweed.

Marvel of Peru

It sat on the table.

That package of seeds. Agatha had always called them four o'clocks back when they sang wild through the woods like banshees, but now apparently they were marvels all the way over in Peru. They grew like weeds, were weeds, they'd had to hack them back each year to make way for the more cowardly violets or the crop plants or the truck garden back when.

They could cover your foot while you stood there, soaking up the sun and rain and just shoving right over your toes to get to the creek across the yard or maybe the lemonade someone was drinking. They did what they wanted, a grabby bunch. But now they were fancy, came in a package, and were no longer named after the time of day when they opened up but after the fancy people in a marvelous place named Peru.

Now that she lived so far away, was so far down the line, no one carried a few seeds around in their hand moist from the day to hand you in case you wanted tomatoes or melons or flowers as nice as theirs. Now, they wanted paper money for seeds and you had to give Caesar his due on top of that. Then, you actually had to plan how and when to plant them. Of all things.

They expected you to check the date and the weather but not the time, as no one planted by the time anymore, not even Mama. She had barely believed in planting at all. Use what's there. You're wasting all His time and effort going to town to buy that. Something even better is already growing right at your feet. She was local back when it was just pure hillbilly not wanting to go to town.

Mama Pearl had also always said each problem has an answer plant growing nearby. When you're bitten by a mosquito, reach down for some mallow. Chew it up like you might for a baby. Then slather the green chaw over the bite, and it will be soothed. She also had answers for snake bites, slow blood and broken hearts, knew the plants with her fingers, her nose and a bit of her eyes. She knew that all mints, wild or tame, were square stemmed. Even the wooly horehound. Even in the dark, she could tell them apart from alfalfa and clover. Not a round stem among them.

If there was no answer plant growing nearby, maybe the problem was just something you needed to learn to live with, plain and simple. That was old talk. But sometimes these things just must be said. If it can't be fixed, maybe wanting to fix it is the problem.

The next thing you knew, Agatha would find poke in a packet, too. Poke that grew alongside every roadway til it was ten feet tall if it liked it well enough. Poke for an evening meal. Pokeberries for ink for sticks to write on the inside bark of trees. Poke switches to chase her brother with. Poke.

Her cousin who went away to school once told her they had even used it to sign the Declaration of Independence. Poke! There was even a parade for it. People came from over and around to say silly things and sing songs and eat poke greens and show off sprigs of poke berries. Some, a few, even sipped at liquor from clear jars.

But there was no parade for four o'clocks even with their fancy new name and painted-up high-rise city apartment called a seed packet.

No, there was no parade for this plant as there was for poke. The flowers were prettier but not ten foot tall. Poke marched everywhere, too, but not back home unless it had already made it there and just kept circling the globe looking for a nice spot to rest in the shade for a moment.

That summer, Agatha reconsidered her beliefs about seed packets and wild weeds and giving Caesar his due and did, in fact, plant her marvels from Peru. She still referred to them as *four o'clocks* as Pearl had. She always had to be back in the yard by the time they opened. That had been fine except for overcast days when they'd opened at the wrong time.

So, Agatha planted them by seeds spread throughout the yard, though admitted only to a patch by the telephone pole, to make it look nice. She might have dropped a few also by the old pecan tree, the new apple tree and some by the funny circle in the grass. It's possible she tossed a few over the fence in all three directions as well. And, perhaps, out by the post office box on the corner. But these might just be lies the townsfolk told to blame her for what was to come.

They grew as plentiful as freckles, and she kept some of the red ones in a jar with spirits to make dye for her jellies. The moths came at night to freshen the flowers and shone darkly on the leaves. There was no need to move the tubers around the yard, as they grew up fresh each year from seed and the roots, both.

At night, the land was drowsy with their scent. Ladies put on their hats and sat outside on their porches just to dream of France or Timbuctoo or maybe Australia. Places where people smelled like this all day long. They wrapped shawls around as it got a little chillier but not much and stretched out their toes to take in the moonlight. The moths swooped down, and the ones with the reddest toenails got a tickle as the moths attempted to say hello.

The marvels ignored Mendel and his science and grew pink colors when they should have only grown red. They grew from their potatoey roots all-round the yard, and they grew from hard black seeds that dropped to the earth and started again next year.

The marvels grew from one yard to the next and then down the block. They brought more moths to the neighbors, big gorgeous moths that no one ever saw when they dove in to feed on the nectar and spread pollen on their legs and wings. No moon moths, these, but larger still, the size of birds who had lost their way at night and begun to howl at the moon and fly about in the bushes.

They shunned the sun and were almost bats, but not quite. They were still paper-thin and wary of anything with sharp beaks who might leave a triangle-shaped hole in one wing, leading to a crashing, a crashing. Edible at heart, they were. Not that big, but still, larger than meadowlarks and certainly larger than chickadees. The few ladies who did see them flying around when the sun had given up soon lost sight of them when the moon napped behind the clouds.

The marvels grew until there was more than one color on each bush. They grew until the laws of nature brushed then bumped then butted heads with the laws of science. But the marvels didn't care. They had never read a textbook made from trees and ink but they had grown under trees and the trees themselves had never uttered a word that said that what the marvels did was impossible.

As with most things in life, when word come up against roots, it's best to side with the dirt because that's where you get your growing from. Words are words and can change with the generations. The marvels gave food and beauty and necklaces the children made in the late afternoon from their yellow flowers.

One day the marvels looked up, and they had grown to the edge of town.

Agatha looked up that day, too, and stopped playing the piano. She put her drink down. She stood up. She walked outside and began to gather all the four o'clocks she could. She picked as many as she could hold, propped them in her hands and along an arm. Then, she went back inside and sat down on the wooden bench, the one with Bicycle Built For Two under the seat.

Agatha took up her needle and thread and began threading flowers into a necklace. She happened to choose all yellows, but she could have mixed them for a pattern or just for pretty. She faced them all this same way but she could have met them in the middle, too. There were so many choices, more than with a bead that was modern and balanced and had no personality but plastic.

A flowerdy necklace would die soon, be smushed flat and sticky in a couple hours, but for those hours, well, plastic or even glass could not do that. You felt the moth wings tittering behind your neck, the sound of the sun in your ears and the perfume on your cheeks. The pink from the flowers was nice for your décolletage, and the yellow ones could even be earrings if you so wanted.

No matter how many Agatha picked, they bumped against each other as far as she could see. The marvels had decided, it seemed, to return to Peru. They marched across the county line and then down by the river. They crossed it on rocks and large tree roots and flat-leaved water plants and on boards that children laid down to cross during high waters. They went up vines and down lawns and in between alleys once they got to the populated areas.

But Peru was further away. It was not just down the road and across the way, it was not the other side of the fence and it was not down near the highway. It was not even across the highway, as one found one day when a seed eaten by a crow landed the other side of the interstate and the march began a new stampede. Well, it was one seed, so stampede is perhaps strong. It was a slow, moment by moment process. The kind of stampede that takes the better part of a decade.

When they did get to the city, they almost hopped a bus, but they had no silver money. So, they began to watch window boxes and rooftop gardens. They went from one to the other and suddenly were up high with the moon and the moths again. Soon, more moths found them, too, and were so dense they covered the moon some nights and even the city, that mean old city, began to smell like an elegant moon.

And there they stayed until their Peru, if was their Peru, would surely come back to them. Would one day look down from the mountains or up from an orchard and run a plank across the open sky for their return. Because plants which can often solve all our heartbreaks can, in fact, in some years, have a bountiful few of their own.

Pearl and Agatha's Marvelous Pink Spirits

Take a few handfuls of four o'clocks--the dark pink ones work best--and soak in a clear spirit like vodka, 'shine or Everclear. If you're fancy, you'll wash them first and then let them dry on towels on the kitchen counter. Actually, that is best so they don't have too much moisture and spoil in the spirits.

Let set for a few days, until the color begins to drain into the liquor. Once that happens, spoon out the flowers, and use the dye in drinks or to lightly color plain gelatin. Nice in lemonade. Can be used in homemade playdough, too, though you may want canned beet juice for that so that you aren't surrounded by drunken children.

Pearl Buts in from the Other Room:

I've heard tell you can do this with poke berries as well, but don't believe them. Those are poisonous. Good for inks, not good for food! If Marvelous Pink Spirits is too fancy for you, you might try making some dandelion wine. You won't need a seed package for that.

Matilda Gets A Chicken

Mr. Tatum had seventeen chickens spread between two enclosures. Each morning at seven and then again at three, he tossed them handfuls of bread, leftover vegetables and stray bits of meat. While he sat smoking his pipe, sometimes he would catch grasshoppers for them by quick dipping his hand off the porch and into the tall grass. He kept them in a jar and when he had a few to merit the effort, would get up off his old bones and totter to the barnyard.

The chickens grew to love grasshopper time and lined up by the tarp eying him through the holes when he began his slow ascent to the hill where they lived. There was a creek just below, and they were uphill as much for sanitary reasons as to prevent them being flooded out on a bad day.

A young girl had moved next door and would watch him through the fence, feeding the chickens. She saw him toss trash on the ground and the poor starving birds ran for it willy-nilly. She saw he did not even bother to put their food properly in a dish. She saw that he drew their water from the mud hole in a dirty old bucket and laid it before them as if it were a splendid feast. She saw them so desperate for food, they ate bugs as their only alternative.

When he went into town, the girl, Matilda, would hop the fence and sit in the long grass to watch the birds. It was her hobby, that and plaiting her hair into long braids. She tried to sneak them food, but only got in trouble as her own family didn't have enough to be sharing with strangers, much less chickens.

She saw them eating rocks and sand and bits of dust and tree bark and sticks and odd blades of grass or weeds. Her mother's chickens came under plastic and rested on Styrofoam, so she had never studied one up close. She had been to school, was, in fact, quite wise for fourteen, but her learning had never taught her much about chickens.

Chickens relish tiny bits of grit and peck the dirt all day long. The crunchy, indigestible bits of hardness grind the food up after it leaves their gullet. At slaughter time, a happy chicken (well, no one is happy at slaughter time, not even the slaughterer) has a belly full of sand and tiny pebbles. Without them, the food would pile up and suffocate them from the inside out.

But there was no textbook meant for a bright fourteen year old that told such tales. And, she was not one to ask questions. She preferred gathering her own information, silently. Her judgments were swift and universal. Bad or Good. She, by the way, was good.

Mr. Tatum had seen the poor family move in next door. He had hoped one of the children would show an interest in the chickens so that, maybe for daily eggs, their mother would send one over to do a bit of the chores. But, they did not seem to need eggs, or did not realize he had chickens. Ten years before, he had gotten his yard mowed plus fresh tomatoes during the season for his lovely brown and sometimes blue-green speckled eggs.

But, he had done nothing more than wave hi to the young family as they drove into the driveway, and maybe that wasn't invitation enough to drop on by as it had been once.

It was getting time to cull for the season. Weed out the one or two he would keep for eggs, maybe an old favorite, and then the rest, would depend. His freezer, or a neighbor's. A chicken in the soup pot for Sunday, or Saturday, depending. Maybe some young child who wanted a pet and whose parents weren't astute enough to know what that would mean over the winter. Trudging out through the snow to feed, knocking ice out of water buckets, the rest. He had a niece who traded the feet to her Chinese neighbor in exchange for glass jars of star anise. So, they would wind up with good homes, in one way or another.

This was not his favorite time of year. But it was a necessary time. It would be like leaving a crop in the field because you could not bear to cut the wheat with a scythe. Wheat might not like to be cut, but humans had stomachs. And stomach aches.

Mr. Tatum took his hat down off the post and got ready for the drive into town. He had considered replacing the tarp but it was so late in the season. Biddy and the one or two others he might keep would go into a smaller enclosure anyway to keep them warm during the coming season.

He thought of picking up ice cream for them next door, but again. Was that too forward? He jingled his keys in his pants pocket as he hopped down the last step. He took the other ones slow to save up the extra oomph for that last signature step of his. It was important to go forth into the world proudly, he felt.

Matilda was eating a bread sandwich when he pulled out of the driveway. She put down the crust. Her mother was not watching, so she hid it in her palm and then in the pocket of her shorts. It was a chilly day, but shorts it was until the next paycheck came through.

She took her book and sidled outside near the fence. No one else in the neighborhood could keep chickens except Mr. Tatum. The rules had changed long ago, but he had been there so long, it didn't matter. Her mother complained of the noise in the mornings when they laid. She didn't know it was their prideful, little look at me dance. She took it to be their *I don't belong here and you can't do anything about it* dance.

Matilda found her mother's good scissors, the ones she used for cutting out patterns. She cut windows for the chickens in the tarp so they could see the day and the sunshine as she did. First one chicken and then another began to perch on the tarp. They clucked at her, unsure of who the stranger was. But, enjoying their fancy new holes, nonetheless. Biddy, and a small, red unnamed one jumped down at once. Perhaps having given each other some secret, it's okay chicken signal. Long ago, Biddy had been in the coop up near the house. And also one down by the creek. She had even spent a night or two inside when she was healing up from a dog bite from a long ago (and now dispatched) neighbor's dog.

She had had a long, if small, life on this quarter acre. She had survived the butchering of the hogs, the coming and going of the seasons, and now she saw the bushes she used to peck by the street the first few years of her life. She was still a bit lame from the dog, so was not allowed out as she used to be to roam here and there. She was more pet than product at this point, as she had produced no eggs in nearly three seasons. She was like the auntie you kept propped in the living room who woke occasionally to say hi to guests or eat her jello after Wheel Of Fortune. You couldn't bear to part with her, but you didn't really expect too much from her, either.

She set off at a trot for the berry bushes, drawn by the color or the shape or perhaps, if chickens can remember that long, a memory. She scooted underneath it to get out of the wind that was picking up and began to snack. The red chicken had given up after a few steps and gone back under the tarp. She didn't like the looks of the girl with the scissors. They were sharp and shiny like a hatchet and she figured she would take her chances with the old man.

Biddy, though, was in her element. Dirt and worms and dried berries littered the ground under the bush. After a bit, she heard Mr. Tatum's standard BEEPBEEP BEEPBEEP, though there had long ceased being anyone at home to greet him. She knew beepbeep beepbeep meant food.

She sailed out from under the bush right under Mr. Tatum's tire. There was a bump, ugly, but not to Mr. Tatum who had merely hit a rock in his driveway. He rolled further up by the porch and unloaded his packages.

Matilda had watched all this, including his early return from next to the blue tarp. She stared at the scissors and tossed them back over the fence, suddenly fearing her mother far more than she did Mr. Tatum. She picked up the largest rock she could find and heaved it again the side of his house. When something fell out of the sky and hit his home, Mr. Tatum went to go see what in tarnation had happened, and Matilda slipped back over to her side of the fence.

When he came back, still puzzled, Mr. Tatum noticed the blood on the front left tire of his car. He was startled the way only an old man can be who has killed enough things on purpose to dread killing something on accident. He paced back down his driveway expecting the carcass of a raccoon, certainly no skunk, as there was no smell. What he saw was Biddy but not Biddy. It was not even a chicken anymore. More of a blob and ants were already starting to form. He vomited on the white gravel like he had never done when processing her sisters for food. He shouted in the language of his German grandparents, not even sure what the words meant, himself, anymore.

He took the handkerchief from his pocket and laid it over her, then went to go get his shovel. As he walked past their fence, he saw Matilda doing homework back there.

"Hey," he said to the girl. "I'm thinking of getting rid of these chickens. Ask your ma if she wants 'em. Either that or they're going in the freezer by tonight". And he went back to bury his friend, not by the bushes as he did not have a long memory and had no idea this was her favorite spot, but over by the lilacs, which to his eye seemed just fine.

Mr. Tatum's Best Ever Yardbird

Homegrown chicken is best. Not only is the flavor better, but the gratefulness you have sticks with you all day long.

Set aside the hen's organs for yourself; those are the cook's own reward. If you'd like to try the gizzard, turn it inside out and dump out the wee, little pebbles and flowers and hay you'll find. Trim off the rubbery muscle after admiring what a strong little thing it is. Fry up the organs first thing to give you stamina for the rest of your cooking. You'll need it.

An old bird will need a little more aging in the fridge first or else a longer, slower cooking time. Remember, a long-lived, well-exercised bird is not exactly a spring chicken. She'll need time to get tender in your pot. A good candidate for marinades, too. If you are a fan of schmaltz or chicken fat, this is usually the hen to get yours from. Be grateful and enjoy!

Third Cousin, Twice Removed on His Mama's Side

It wasn't me what killed him. That was the peanut butter sandwiches. And, maybe the drugs. Me, I was a flea. Smaller. The gentleman with the hair dye. At his funeral.

His casket. Oh, that casket. You never seen. I wouldn't have wanted one like it. Well, I would've. Who wouldn't have? Should've said, can't-won't have. You know. Too much.

My daddy's own casket was green. The cheapest one. The one they sell you in the prepaid plan so when your relatives come in later they rebuy you a whole other one as you are laid out real pretty in a box made from a picnic table at the county park. But, us, we let him keep it that way. Green isn't that ugly. To me.

I did that day, six weeks later, what I should have had the gumption to do at my daddy's own funeral. My cousin's hair was done up nice. He had his own hairdresser. Being famous gets you that. But it was white. Too much. He didn't like gray, who does? It was funny around the sides. He wouldn't have liked it. He would've liked a little grease, even at the end. I had something in the car. It smells funny but works fast.

I went and got a glass of water first. Then I sidestepped my way out to the Buick and opened the tailgate right up. I got out my box of whatnots. Tools and this and such and that. Amid the thats and this's was some shoe polish, nice and black. Shiny.

I stuffed it in my left pocket and ambled back in. I could smell it through the tin like a big factory warehouse of new, just gleaming from my pocket. We were gonna newify him if it was the last thing I did.

In the sitting parlor, I got another glass of water. This time, they had ice. I took my handkerchief and dabbed it with polish. Not sure I should be putting something from my shoes right up near his face. I went at the hairline, mostly, but also the sides. They really needed freshening up. Dying may be something you have to put up with, fine, but dying with gray hair is a whole other matter.

It improved his smell. I must say that. Now he was not perfumey, not powdery. What man would want that? Nor moldering. He was full of new car smell, the latest and greatest just off the line in Detroit. A caddy headed for the highway on a smooth cross country trip that wouldn't feel a pothole, one.

I got some under my nails that day. Wound up with a tiny trickle down my own pale forehead from where I wiped my face in the heat. I was wearing my best blue suit with the mother of pearl snaps that day. And my three corner hat. Me and Elvis Aaron, I have to tell you, we both looked good at his funeral.

The Third Cousin's Peanut Butter and Banana Sandwich

Start with your brand of peanut butter and a nice, ripe banana.

Depending on your raising and your circumstance, you may next add Karo clear corn syrup, wild honey, backyard honey, pancake syrup, sugar cane molasses or real maple syrup. A bit of cinnamon or nutmeg is good also, though you're going a bit rogue here.

You can eat it like this as a sandwich, on toast or fry it up on some nice bread. Some use butter or oleo, others just a dry, hot skillet. Either way, the best taste comes from cast iron without a doubt. Yes, you can use other metals, I understand, but what better skillet is there that can also be used in self-defense?

The Third Cousin Confesses His Unfair Dislike of Natural Peanut Butter:

Of course, you may also use natural peanut butter and no syrup at all. But, please keep that to yourself.

Joe Potato

The winter was killing the farm. Not even the spiders had food. They shriveled up like the sucked dry carcasses already spun in their webs and fell to the floor gradually in little, silent breaths.

The man, Joe Potato, and his wife, Marjorie, were young while also being old. Their shirts were blue, like their neighbors', and their boots were tan. Their hair was combed back to look shorter than it was. At night, they let it hang down freely in the farmhouse, not worried then about looking too frivolous or prideful of their manes.

Marjorie would pat out flat bread for the griddle as she undid her barrette. Or, begin patting out the bread in her mind, always a step ahead of herself with chores. Joe was less rushed, much like his family name perhaps. He was solid, but a bit sluggish. His skin was over-white, while Marjorie's was the outside of the potato, a nice brown from the sun.

Any children they had would have been known as small fries, they both knew and somehow, their pride kept them from procreating. It was unspoken but true. They had both been teased as children, he for the obvious and she for a mole just above her lips. Neither wanted that for their own. Or, rather, perhaps, neither could imagine comforting a child each evening after school as they themselves had had to be comforted for over twelve years.

"Joe, can you come help with the bread?"

That summer had been fruitful. Literally. But then snow had come early and hard and had shattered all plans of a nice potato harvest. They froze in the ground. Later, they were dug up for home use but were useless for the market or even for trade. They didn't mind the mealiness themselves, but others would.

They kept rabbits in the barn for times like these. They ate the meat themselves or bartered it with neighbors. A man down the road came on Saturdays to do chores just so he could eat a good midday meal with them. Marjorie felt it was the best he had all week and always sent him home with extras.

This week she was uncertain. A man working for food, and she with none to give, yet too embarrassed to phone him. The phone had been disconnected once due to her pride, her inability to tell the woman on the line that she needed to pay in installments, please.

She paid it in full two days later, but they had already incurred a large fee which they only just got paid off this summer. Joe's pride was different. He more cared about his TV being polished and no dust on the window sills. That was it for him. Oh, and a swept-clean step. That was it.

"Can you run down and tell Chuck we can't afford him this weekend?"

He chewed his tobacco thoughtfully, with an eye toward the television.

"That boy hates me. He'll just think I don't want him around anymore after he talked to your sister like that."

"No, he won't. Go tell him we want him, we just can't afford him this week."

She knew it would be another month but she was trying to keep hope.

"Oh, let him come. You can always find something."

"There is nothing. Go tell him."

"You made me ask for more credit at the market on Tuesday. Where did that go?"

"In your stomach. You can't let him come here to work and go home with nothing!"

He ignored her and went back to the television.

She eyed the door to the barn that connected through the laundry room. Her favorite rabbit had just had kits. To use her now would kill that litter too. They would need a few more weeks with her to get a good start.

She could hear their mewing through the door, though actually she couldn't. They didn't mew. Their faces looked like they would but they didn't. The main sound they made or, really, that Patsy the mother rabbit made, was a low bark, just like a dog, when taken out of the crate unawares. Normally she liked to be picked up; in fact, the dog came and licked her though the wood. Patsy leaned into the dog's licks the way you might a warm shower after a hot day. She would be a hard one to eat.

"Joe, really. I need you to go down and talk to him. I can't."

He flicked the channel and did not look up.

"Really, I meant it. Go tell him. I can't."

She wiped her hands on the apron. Both were still clean; she hadn't started chopping yet. He twisted his neck a smidgen. Just enough to let her know she was being ignored, but good.

She went to the fridge. There was cauliflower that had greyed with mildew. She shaved the spots off and added some margarine to a pan and began dinner. She dug into her palm just a small bit with the knife. An indentation, no blood. She exhaled. She searched around the back of the fridge til she found some peas as a treat for Patsy.

A penance for tomorrow's duty. She could put the babies in the grinder for the dog, small bones and all. He would never eat his friends knowingly, but in a round bowl on the floor with warm water to make gravy, they would serve up fine.

Mrs. Potato's Rabbit Supper

Once you've skinned and cleaned out your rabbit, marinate in ½ bottle of whatever vinegared salad dressing you like. Fill up most of the rest of the pot with water. If it's from the creek, boil it first. It hasn't been the same out there since Mama died.

Let set in the fridge for a good three days, if possible. You can add herbs, too, if you are that kind of person. When it's nice and done, cook up as usual. I prefer a quick cook, as it's awfully lean and can't stand much cooking. If you want to give it a long cook, use a bit of oil to help it along. Much drier than hamburger or chicken, otherwise. A quick cooking is best, though, all the way around. Saves the flavor and does good by the rabbit.

The Troll of Mustard Creek Bridge

Mr. Irish Johnston kept his pocketknife close by on full moon evenings. These were the best nights for walks along the river bank. No fish to speak of, just minnows. But, his neighbor enjoyed hanging her feet off the bridge over her creek. And he liked his neighbor. Well, liked is a strong word. He more liked to whittle as he watched her dip her toes in the cool evening water.

He brought his flashlight along most evenings. It was strong and had a nice heft to it. A watchman's flashlight. Almost a spotlight. He also brought rope, as you never knew when you might need it. Duct tape, too, as it was awfully handy. Really, he had a whole backpack he kept of supplies, just in case. He kept his white cap in there as well as his extra shoes. And a new belt with a fine, shiny buckle. It said RODEO on it in big letters.

His great uncle had rodeoed, not him, but he liked the look of it. It said something to folks who liked the way it glinted in the light. Miss Southern, Ann Southern, was the gal who liked to dip her toes in the moonlight. A splash of water up against her ankles wasn't bad either. Good antidote to the too long days at work and after putting the kids to bed.

She, too, had a pocketknife that she kept with her on moonlit nights. She was not proud of hers in the way Irish was, but Miss Southern knew how to use hers just as well. She also knew how to swing an axe but liked the curve of the handle of her pocketknife and the way it fit in her hand. An axe was rather forward, she felt. She had been raised not to be forward or obvious in her attentions, to be lady-like no matter what the cost.

What this caused was a preparation on her part that was part innocent and part single woman who enjoyed sitting alone in the moonlight. She was young, though tall, with slightly buck teeth. Or, what would have been called buck teeth. People were too polite to use such a term these days. Both her children had inherited this feature. The family loved corn on the cob, which was perhaps God's little joke and perhaps just the sheer joy of using those big teeth to do what they were meant to do.

It was a Saturday night, and Miss Southern had slipped down by the creek for her nightly moment alone. The children were just up the hill in bed with the door locked. The mastiff snuggled up under the covers with them, as good a mother as you might find. This was what Miss Southern needed, to dip her feet in the water and lean back on her wooden bridge. That, and a cola at her hip, in a bottom-heavy glass that was difficult to knock over in the dark.

She had come down here seventeen nights in a row. Her neighbor, she couldn't help but notice, turned off his lights and edged his screen door open shortly after she made her descent. He was friendly but awkward during the day. At night, he was more forward, and it did not become him.

She had brought a hardboiled egg in her pocket, and she tapped it on the bridge. She should have brought a salt shaker but had not considered that. The yolk was creamy and large, the way homegrown eggs were. The yellow showed up dark gray in the moon, but in the sun it would have been a yellow's yellow. Chickens who stretched their legs and fetched their own greens from the yard as blades of grass or random weeds always made prettier eggs, and hers were no exception.

Irish knew this and helped himself to hers when she left for work each day. She would have gladly shared with him, but Irish didn't want them to eat. He wanted them to have. He coveted things that weren't his, and asking for them would have ruined their taste in his tinny mouth. He preferred pepper to salt, and sometimes ate them with a mouthful of hot sauce. He needed things to burn or he could not enjoy them. Had always been that way since he was a boy.

The neighbor then had been an old gentleman who grew the neighborhood's best tomatoes. He ate one during the season every day on the way to school. He had never asked then, either, as even at that young of age asking took all the pleasure out of it for him.

The doctors had diagnosed him about this when he was seven and then again at thirteen when he had pulled off his cat's nails with pliers. But that doctor had moved away for better pay, and few people remembered that now. Irish no longer had those pliers, he had buried them with a host of other things out behind his cabin. He kept a pile of rocks and leaves over it, tending it the way someone else might a baby. His real tools, his special tools, were close at hand but also easily hidden. Well, maybe not easily, but, again, that was part of Irish's joy. The stealth of love. Or, not love. What was the word?

He liked his tools the way others might love their morning coffee. Something he could not function without, even if it was not fit conversation for polite company. He kept them at the ready for the right moment as others might a tray of creamer, sweetener and spare coffee cups for unplanned visitors. He kept his for unplanned moments which could never properly present themselves unless one planned beforehand to the extent that Irish was known for. Or, not known for, except for by his long-gone cat. And the doctor. Who had moved away.

Miss Southern was still missing the taste of salt when the hairs on her arm, just under the cuff of her summer shirt, noticed Irish's approach. Her ears didn't recognize him. They often did. He would purposefully make a little cough. Sometimes to let her know he was there politely, and sometimes to test to see if she recognized his presence. He had a different smile prepared for each situation.

Not hearing his cough, nor seeing his favorite belt buckle glint, she knew he was there with a different sort of mission that night. It was when she could not hear him that she was most aware of his presence. His need for control was so focused that he sometimes forgot that even those under observation could observe as well. Sometimes your chicken dinner on your plate wakes up and looks back up at you. Not often, and sometimes only in drunken dreams, but it does happen on occasion.

Irish, to his credit, was not drunk that night. Nor had he smoked any of his nephew's funny cigarettes. His mind was clean and clear. The night air seeped into this lungs a bit at a time as he did his best to breathe as quietly as possible. He could hear the cicadas and hoped that their noise would cover any of his own.

Miss Southern had by now finished her egg and washed it down with her soda. It was not a good flavor combination, but it would do to get the dry out of her mouth. She set her no-spill cup down three inches to her left, which happened to be just where Irish's foot had come to rest as a cloud passed over the moon. The cup, unbalanced, fell over backwards. Irish, who had wanted to make a good first impression, accidentally stepped backwards out of instinct so as not to lose his balance himself.

Miss Southern pulled for his ankle but got his boot. The leather was just old enough, with enough to give to allow her the tiniest finger hold. She jerked with all her might and to both their surprises, Irish found himself hanging over the bridge. It was not a steep drop by any means and not one that would actually be scary, if it were not that it had happened to him by surprise and in the pitch dark of night as the cloud passed in front of his normally friendly moon.

His hand grabbed for her, or anything, really, that would settle his feet back on dry ground. He found her hair and then his claw scraped her face. She made use of her God-given talents, and Irish, who had always liked burning sensations, for once found one he didn't like. Even in the not light, he knew that his hand was now dripping bright, hot red.

Miss Southern hopped back out of instinct and left Irish twirling, trying to find his way back up on the bridge. She chewed for a moment on the appendage the way one might a toothpick. It was rubbery, and not tasty, but satisfying the way a zucchini you had grown yourself over a long hot summer might be.

She reached down to pick up his flashlight that galumphed to her side. The fingernail was clean, for a man's, and the knuckle bony from arthritis and hard work. She stood up to walk back, then on second thought, ran back home. She had separated her neighbor from one of his favorite parts, and it was possible he might want it back.

The noise in the yard had woken the mastiff. There was a satisfying crunch as he sat for his snack and a pat on his head, good boy. The mastiff was used to the large beef bones from the extra freezer where Miss Southern stored her meat. A man's knuckle bone was not as much of a treat, but it was fresh and from his mistress, so the animal was appreciative, as always.

A sleepy voice called from the landing, "Mama, what was the noise?"

"Oh, sweetie, that was just Jonesy wanting a midnight snack."

The child, sleepy, went back in and rolled back over. The moon came back out from behind the clouds and shone on his face through the window. His blue eyes were not their true blue this time of the night, but when Miss Southern stepped into his room from the hallway, she recognized them as her own. She cracked the window for a little night air, the first time she'd felt able to since they'd moved in. She wasn't quite ready to take the bars off, but this was a start.

Tomorrow they would have corn for dinner as a treat. She could taste the butter and the ice tea. Maybe a picnic on the bridge. With potato salad. All sides and no main dish. She was not hungry for meat, and the children preferred their starches anyway. Maybe even a blanket for a tablecloth. And, a big, beef bone for Jonesy. Tonight was just the hors d'oeuvres.

Ann Southern's Starches for Lunch

Some days all you want for lunch is a nice starch. Potatoes come in handy here, mashed, baked or as a salad. Or, be fancy, and do a German potato salad that's a bit warm and tangy. You know the kind, with a nice, strong mustard. (If you are the type to gather wild mustard seeds off tumble mustards or similar greens, now you know where you can use them!)

If you happen to have a nice set of teeth, corn is nice to keep them busy with so they don't get to jabberjawing all day long. Just don't overcook it. Mushy corn may not be a sin, but it's not a blessing either.

Other good starches are rice cooked however you like and also black-eyed peas. If you put them together, you've got Hopping John, beans and rice, or whatever you call it in your neck of the woods. Hominy's not too bad either, but some don't care for it too much. I'll let you decide on that one.

Serve them all at once on a nice picnic afternoon, and you'll have a sleepy summer Sunday, and, really, what could be better than that?

Miss Southern bends over to whisper:

If your dog is feeling a might peckish and needs a treat, consider Malachi's meat jello for dogs (page 48).

Eating Crow

The man tipped his water over when the commotion started. It drenched the dandelions and melted their wishes far down into the dark green of the alfalfa and plantain. A coyote was stalking the chickens. It had given up, though, the day was too hot, and settled on a black bird sitting high up, but not enough, in a tree.

One moment the bird's almost prehistoric black talons were gripping the branch, and the next moment it gave not even a caw. The music had stuck somewhere in its throat. What the man heard was an almost sound, the kind of sound something makes when it's too desperate to even breathe.

He did not know it was a wild bird. He sent the dog, his dog, over to chase the animal away. In a moment, there was a snap, and the cow dog, the good cow dog, was hobbled. Then the coyote, or what passed for a coyote from far away, was gone down the trail. Mid-sprint, he dropped the black bird. Perhaps out of penance, but more probably out of the instinctive knowledge that keeping his prey might instigate more of a chase than leaving it behind.

So, one hungry beast ran off, one poor dead one lay on the ground, and a hobbled one sniffed it then ran up on the wooden porch. The man took off his hat, cussed his water glass, and went to see after the hobbled one.

Inside, the dog went to its favorite chair, really everyone's favorite chair, and sat down. It was the only plump chair in the room and high enough off the ground to avoid drafts in the winter and see out the window in the summer.

The man dug in the cabinet for medicine, both kinds. One for the wound and another to draw up in a syringe, the ones he'd bought for a quarter and kept in plastic for in case.

There was no antibiotic in the fridge next to the milk, nor had it gotten moved by mistake down into the vegetable crisper. There was none.

The vet was closed and even if open, far too expensive for the man in the brown hat to afford. His teeth spoke that for him even if his words did not.

He dug in his pocket for the ten dollars the antibiotics would cost and set off for the feed store. He reached there before closing and by the time he returned home, the vial had returned to room temperature, which was best for giving shots, not cold and straight from their medicine fridge.

The dog would not know this was a good thing. Does anyone ever believe their own pain is a good thing? After settling the dog with pats in the chair, he swooshed some of the powder into the wound. Then he withdrew liquid into the syringe, put a hand on the dog's collar so he did not get bit, himself, by the frightened old beast, and pushed the gray needle into the dog's fur.

He also injected, in some ways, the gas money he would have used going to the store for food and the few dollars for bread and bologna he would have likely spent. He thought about this on the way home from the feed store and pondered it over a beer after he once again settled the dog with a pat.

On the third pat, he picked up his cap once more, set the brim, and walked out the door and down the path to where the coyote had dropped the black bird. It was still warm, and he picked it up by the feet the way he might have a chicken and let it dangle as he walked.

Inside he cut off the talons as a sort of talisman, against what or for what he was not sure. But surely the shiny blackness of it would bring something good. He looked at the dog and spoke with his hands, the way his mother, also deaf, had taught him.

He began to fix it the way he would a chicken, reaching in to gather the small heart in his hands, somewhat surprised that a liver still looks like a liver no matter who it first belonged to. He found the gizzard, too, though was it still called that? Sometimes things changed names over the years or in different animals. To himself, he named it a gizzard.

He cut the meat up with scissors, the same he might use for paper. It was much easier on his hands than a knife. To chop with a knife, he needed to also pound the blade with a hammer. His hands would no longer do that type of strong work for him.

They were strong enough to keep his promise to the dog, though, to cook up a dinner of the culprit's bird since he could not afford a trip to the next city over for a vet. The old boy would not know where his dinner came from, but it would soothe the man in a way that keeping ten dollars in his pocket til tomorrow for proper food would not.

The skillet was hot before he put in the oil, and then the oil just about smoked before he added the bird. He had sliced off the part with the coyote bite in case as there was some sort of poison or germ or something in the fang mark that could harm him or the dog. He had considered rabies, he knew about that. But consoled himself with the idea that an animal mad with rabies would not be wise enough to snag a bird nearly out of the sky as the coyote had.

Whether it was true or not, time would tell. But in the meantime, there was television, some supper for the table, and maybe a crossword. He walked over to set his favorite pencil and a sharpener by the plump chair. Then he hovered over the dog to pick it up. He would let the dog eat in place tonight. But, not tomorrow.

Then he could sit with the man in the truck as they sat in the yard, listened to the A.M. radio, and maybe even shot pellets at cans. Under the seat, as always, there would be a margarine tub of dog food and a beer, warm, but just right for the day.

Frying Crow

Most fresh meat is tastier after it's been let to set a few days in the fridge. Fresh meat is tougher than supermarket meat, because it hasn't aged yet. That's the main difference. To eat the same day, slice into small pieces about the size of fried okra. Cooking too large a piece will make it tough to chew. Toss in a paper bag with seasoned flour or cornmeal. Drop into a very hot skillet with oil. Will cook in just a few moments. Good eaten with black coffee, as hot as you can stand it, and a salad of young dandelion greens on the side. If you are fancy, fry up some of the dandelion flowers at the same time as the bird. They may not taste like yellow but they still sort of feel like it.

If you want to eat a flower that tastes like what you think it might, try wild violets sprinkled with sugar. Smells nice. Good on a salad or even oatmeal. Or, pick henbit. Let your whole side yard go to henbit if you ever get the chance. Useful as a green, too. If you find yourself in the middle of a wild strawberry patch, pick a few handfuls. No bigger than the tip of your pinky. Perfect to eat right then and make you glad for the day or bring home and toss with the sugar and violets. Or, mix in a salad. You won't be disappointed.

If you're a gardener, try the purpley white flowers on your oregano. Some call it marjoram.

The Man adds:

Best to just eat wild greens and flowers. Or fruits. The chickens just ruin your garden anyway.

Malachi Jones

It started when Malachi was eight and he taught his poodle Francine to dance. The dog learned to prance on two feet and stretch her front legs to Malachi's hands. It wasn't the waltz, and it wasn't the mambo, but it would do for them.

Malachi sang Pennies From Heaven, though the dog just heard a crackling noise that meant, no one's talking about food right at the moment. That year, Francine got pregnant through a consensual rendezvous with the pit bull next door.

Mr. Jones, Malachi's father, got angry. "I don't get home til midnight just trying to feed you." He gave Malachi the kind of look that said, even for a frail eight year old you eat too much.

So Malachi began thinking. He wanted to see the pups, but how would they pay for the food? What if Francine needed an operation like their corner neighbor did? Drowning them would be a cruel waste, he knew that from the TV.

That Thursday before payday when they ate the heel of the bread, it came to him. They could eat the puppies. He was so proud, he sat up so straight his backbone nearly popped. He sneaked Francine more food from the table than usual to fatten her and the puppies up.

He hugged her in bed that night. "Just wait. Dad can't complain if you're bringing us food instead of taking it away. You'll be our little dancing cow." He squeezed her and looked deep in her eyes.

Francine laid her head on his pillow and snuggled her nose behind his ear, where it fit just in the space Mr. Jones had accidentally cut when he was trimming Malachi's hair the evening he heard about the puppies to be. It had that nice healing smell that older wounds did, and she licked it and sniffed it til they both fell asleep soothed by the routine.

As Francine got rounder, the boy got prouder. He would show her off to the neighbors like a prize sow. He had never been proud of anything in his life, and it was unusual of him to brag this way. Every time someone said that dog of yours sure is getting fat, he pulled his shoulders back YES SHE IS. And he beamed at her and she back at him.

He began to look through random magazines for recipes for puppies. He looked in the waiting room at the doctor and at his friend Bobby's house when he went over to spend the night.

"Do you have any dog recipes?" he asked Bobby's mother.

"Well, 1 think there's a recipe for dog bones over by the record player. My grandmother used to always take old bones, make soup and then let 'em have it afterwards. She called it dog bone soup." She laughed and thought of her mom's mom putting the beef bones in the tall pot and the nice smell it brought into the house.

"The marrow is the best," she said.

"The absolute best. The marrow. Okay. Thanks." He wasn't sure what marrow was, but his dad would have to be happy with anything that was the absolute best? And dog bones had it. The marrow. He tried to think of words that rhymed with it so he wouldn't forget it.

He walked back in the room and asked her to write it down on a piece of paper for him. "Sure," she said and whisked off the word marrow in just a moment's time, not slow and long like it took his dad, who sometimes just handed the paper back empty with a glare.

He had been going to wait til the big day itself but found that he couldn't. It was like holding back a surprise party when you just have to spill the beans to someone, no matter who.

When his dad got home that night, Malachi was waiting up for him. "I figured out what to do with the puppies. I got a recipe. We make marrow from them. It's the best. Bobby's mom said so." He said this all in one breath and then stepped out of the way in case the mention of the word puppy caused a swing of Mr. Jones' arm before he could hear the good news.

The man was tired from the factory, but his gray face at midnight still had enough blood in it to turn bright red in outrage. "EAT THE PUPPIES. You little profaner. What are you talking about? You can't eat them damn puppies. You're a profaner. You're a profaner. That's what you are. A profaner."

He was too discombobulated to punch Malachi much less spit on his proud kitchen floor. He kept spinning around, literally, his toes doing a dance he remembered from when Malachi's mother was still alive. Daddy Loves Mambo was going through his head. He sat down for the first time in twelve hours. "EAT THE PUPPIES?"

By this time Malachi knew he had done something wrong, but he wasn't sure how. His dad had fairly toppled into the chair no one sat in, the one the Grandmother who said Malachi was a Bible word for messenger said keep open for company. He had planned to parade Francine in front of his father, showing off her chubby tummy, and now he wasn't so sure.

He kept out of arm's reach as he asked, "What's a profaner?" Did *pro* mean he was good at it?

"Go look it up," his dad said.

"Where? We don't have a dictionary."

"Well, go find one!"

Malachi took the leash, the best one with the purple cloth and the diamonds on the handle and took Francine for a walk to the marrow lady's house to borrow one. It took him two blocks to realize it was midnight, his errand was so important. So he went to the park and sat under a poplar tree listening to the leaves make music with each other. And Malachi Jones waited til morning.

Malachi's Meat Jello for Francine (Two Kinds)

Grandma says she doesn't know about Francine, but her old dog liked meat jello best. Good for its old bones when the weather was acting up. I say, "Grandma, what about your old bones?" but then she picks up the flyswatter so I stop. It prickles.

She used to boil extra bones (possum mostly but also cow when she had it) for hours. And then a little more. So, put as many bones as can fit in your biggest pot, boil it to Jesus, boil it a little more, then put the juicy water out for the dog. Yum. It'll grease up its joints good. (You could wait til it sets a little but why? It can set up later in their stomach. I don't like to wait, me. Eat it while it's still good.)

If you're fancy, put the broth in a coffee can, add plain jello with no flavor, yeast for beer and then, if you have it, stinky cheese. If you go in for pizza, take those little packets of parmesan cheese. Those'll work good.

Stick it in the icebox or on the windowsill to cool, she says. When it looks like meat jello, give it to the dog, don't eat it. People don't eat things left to set in coffee cans anymore. But, I think it's good. You can't keep your drippings on the back of the stove in the metal coffee can anymore either, but why not? I like her cornbread made from that better than made with oleo.

That store-bought jello will take the weather out of their bones, the beer yeast is good for the flea itch, and the stinky cheese is because dogs like anything that smells like your feet.

And, for you, in case you have old bones, too, save the possum grease for yourself. Rub it in with just itself or add what you like to it. Brings warmth. Add ground cayenne for extra heat, but beware the color on your clothes or sheets.

Two Sides to Every Story

"Ma? What kinda cancer did Aunt Sugar have?"

"She didn't have any cancer."

"Oh. I thought she hadda couple kinds a cancer?"

"No. She had arthritis."

"She didn't have a couple kinds a cancer? Back when she stayed with us?"

"Well, she had mouth cancer and then she did have lung cancer. But it was only two kinds. It wasn't like she had a lot of it."

Back when Aunt Sugar was busy not having cancer, she would be gone from our home for days at a time. When she returned, we fed her broth and were very quiet. It was the days before remotes, when children were the channel changers. They sat by the TV like the ball boys at a Wimbledon tennis match, at the ready to go and change to whichever of the three available channels the reigning adult needed.

Her favorite was the news. If it ended on one station, we were to search until we found it on the next. As this required only three flips until you were back again, you tried to make them very long flips, turning the knob very slowly to dial in the channel a bit at a time. As soon as she saw a movie or Dialing For Dollars, you would have to begin flipping all over again. The white noise pictures in between the channels became a stopping place, a hanging-out place before her disappointment appeared again.

Since no adults changed their own channels in those days, except for, I suppose, those without children within arm's reach, it was not strange to us. I remember setting up camp on especially bad days, putting my soda under the TV on the floor so as not to mar the TV, itself. I'm not sure that TVs were marrable in those days, but we felt they were. Just as we felt that a doily was good for the back of every chair not to mention the arms of the nicer ones.

My brother came in one day while I was dialing the TV stations in as slowly as I could. Aunt Sugar was asleep, but I knew that as soon as I stopped switching channels she would open one eye and tell me to begin again. So, we passed the Million Dollar Movie and Don Mahoney and Jeanna Claire in their spangly cowboy outfits, then came back to the man calling people at home live on TV. If they answered, they won seven dollars. If they weren't home, he began again, and this time the jackpot increased. This was when gambling was only in Las Vegas, and some people even refused to play bingo at church. It was, I mean, a bit risqué. The lights flashed all around his head, and you know that Miranda on 12th Street would be told by all her neighbors that she had missed the Lucky Seven jackpot that day by taking her sweet time at the grocery store.

My brother said he had got out the braunschweiger (which was my father's food) for us to eat while he was at work. Both my parents worked Saturdays. He sliced it off in little bits. It was terrible, worse than our fried bologna sandwiches that we usually had. I tucked mine down in the cat's dish, where it was gone instantly.

"Why are you eating this? It tastes like crap."

"Because he says we can't."

"Well, then, grab a beer while you're at it!"

We both eyed them up on the shelf. Then we saw the Kool-Aid packets my mom used for daiquiris and decided to make a glass of lemonade.

"She'll kill us."

"Yeah, but not like him."

I got down the pitcher and made the lemonade. He was halfway into the braunschweiger before he realized. We looked at each other, and he put it right back where it was.

"Get out the baloney!"

He fried us up two sandwiches each, carefully using up both heels of the bread so that at least one of our sandwiches wouldn't count. If you used the parts of food no one else liked, then you got a freebie with our parents.

"You know why she's in there, don't you?"

"Whaddya mean? Watching TV?"

"No. I mean, you know why she's in there, right?" He got annoying when he repeated himself word for word.

"Sleeping?"

"No, I mean you know WHY she's in there, right?"

"To get better?" I had a vague idea she was sick, but since she never asked for Kleenex, I let it be.

"Her lips are broken. Dad told me."

"Whaddya mean, they're broken?"

"A doctor cut them off. She got cancer from the snuff."

"The chaw? You mean the chaw made her sick?"

"Yeah, it gave her cancer. So they cut them off." I pictured my mother's kitchen scissors cutting a section out of my aunt's face. I looked at him.

"What did they do with them?" I pictured the pickled pigs feet on the counter at the Seven Eleven.

"How do I know? But you know what they put in their place? Dad told me last night when they were playing poker."

I never got to stay up on poker nights, but my brother got to empty ash trays, throw away pop tops and wipe up vomit around the toilet. He was happy to for the chance to stay up and learn men stuff.

"They cut off her you know and replaced it up there."

I didn't know. "Her head? They cut off her head?"

"NO."

I tried to think of all the you knows I could think of. "Her boobs? They cut off her boobs?"

"No, you idiot. For crying out loud. They cut off her YOU KNOW." He pointed to where my green corduroys came together in the center.

"Her that? No way. How does she pee?"

"I don't know." For once he looked thoughtful instead of like a know-it-all. "I'll have to ask...." he stopped. "No. He won't tell me. I only heard because he was telling Mr. Ramirez. The one that never smokes."

I knew which one he was. He parked on our lawn, and I always had to pull the sprinkler hose out from underneath his wheels before he drove off in the mornings, because it was my job to sprinkle the lawn before school. He was usually asleep in his car. But he had learned to keep the windows up, as it always seemed to rain in the morning at our house.

I snuck back in to look at my aunt's face. I'd never noticed it before. To me, it was an old lady's face. She was twenty-nine and so old she creaked. I was scared to get closer than the foot of the couch. I tried to see if her face looked any different than it did before. It was sort of puffy. But all grown-ups looked like that in the morning. I got the tiniest bit closer and thought I could see a mark down by the corner of her mouth. Maybe it was not a Marilyn Monroe mark like I thought. Maybe that was the part they cut off. Maybe that was the part they patched up.

I ran back to tell my brother. "She has a funny scab in the corner. Is that what you mean? Did I see it? Did I see it?"

He looked at me. "No, idiot, it's all healed up. That's why she was able to come home. Dad says you can't tell at all except for when you kiss her."

"Kiss her? When did dad ever kiss Aunt Sugar? She socked him in the gut for just touching her toothbrush in the bathroom."

He had his I-get-to-stay-up-late-and-empty-ashtrays-and-hear-men-talk look again. I ran back to where she was sleeping. The cat had curled up right behind her knees under the black afghan with the stretchy holes in it. One ear poked out next to a periwinkle flower. They were both in the fetal position, both enjoying those last few moments before awakening.

I took my sandwich apart and went and sat next to her. The smell didn't wake her. The bologna was curled up into a little cup, and it held the grease just perfectly the way I liked. I took the tiniest sip then put it back on my sandwich. There was a movie on where Santa Claus fights Martians. I moved her chapstick to the side, stretched out my toes and settled in.

The Two Kids' Fried Baloney Sandwiches (much better than braunschweiger, believe you me)

Fry the baloney up, then either place it on toast or plain bread. If you're fancy, you can also finish it like a grilled cheese sandwich by placing the bread in the skillet, too. You can use Miracle Whip or just enjoy the warm grease as its own wonderful condiment. No matter which camp you belong to, however, this is not a baloney and cheese sandwich. Do not even dare.

Mr. Martinez gives his two cents:

If you use good quality, natural bologna, what exactly is the point of this recipe? You might as well have a steak alongside it. Works best with the greasiest baloney you have.

Good on the stove but safer for kiddos in the microwave. And, still curls up into its own little bowl.

Aunt Sugar wakes up in time to give her opinion on fried baloney cups:

Some folks will tell you to slice a bit out of the baloney first so it doesn't curl up. But, that is high treason. Who does not need a tiny cup of grease in their day? Warms your belly and soothes your soul like nothing else.

Winter's Coming

The first doll Uncle Son saw when he peeked in the waist-high window had corn silk hair and a skirt from striped corn husks. Not strippy stripes, bold and you can't stand to look at them, but nice, almost hidden pin stripes, the kind corn husks get when dried. Or, drier. These had been molded and folded a bit until they really did mimic a skirt and the top two bent a bit sideways til they made arms waving at him or maybe up at a star tilting too far to the left toward heaven. You don't even want to know about the second doll.

The second doll had an apple core head, dried to brown perfection and sweetened with age until the nooks and crannies in her face resembled, if not a real grandma, at least one a bit more realistic than one made out of a banana. You laugh, but a banana would make a terrible doll.

The third doll was an old pantyhose filled with cotton or an old shirt or something soft and stained but no matter as you can only see enough to see inside hose to know you can't see what it really is. Someone had drawn a needle through the hose to bend it down for a chin and a nose and then sewn cracks and a forehead and, finally, well, it did look like a lady. And not even one with pantyhose on her head. One a bit tired that had a hard day and was finally able to sit down with her coffee just before midnight and was glad for it.

You should know that there was also doll furniture made out of Pabst Blue Ribbon cans that could be seen through the early-winter window. Now, perhaps you want me to say root beer or cream soda cans, but truly, well, they were beer cans because those were made of much sturdier stuff. They were cut and bent and trilled into curves and wherves and whirls. The edges were singing, if metal edges of a twirled beer can chair can sing. Any doll in her right mind would be tickled to sit in them, but the owner found them best to display just for themselves.

These were the dolls and doodads and dandifieds you met as you peered through the curtain into the kitchen. There were more, but those were hidden in other rooms and best left for other days.

Tipping back on his heels, Uncle Son began to wonder if this person was the right person to borrow his home from this winter. But who was better than an old lady who made dolls and was obviously gone for the season by the way no car had seen the driveway for several days.

He went to the side near the back garden by the second rock and got the key. He searched around for a few minutes and finally actually found it by the seventh rock in the front garden by the farthest front window. He had a mental metal file cabinet of who kept what where that he searched on occasion to know where something he needed just might be in a stranger's life.

Stepping into the kitchen, he took a breath of cigarettes and Pine Sol and...no, not Brut. Something manly like that. Maybe she hadn't always lived alone. He looked on the counter for cookies or snacks or something left behind at the last minute, something that no one would look for next year when they came back to prepare for the warm season.

But there was nothing. The apple headed doll was quite dried and might do in an actual emergency, but he was old enough to know that sleeping in a stranger's house for three months was not an emergency but life, plain and simple.

So he began, as was his way, to unpack. His toothbrush by the kitchen sink. He was not much of a bathroom person. A bit scary, to be in the behind of someone's house if they came in suddenly. Toothbrushing was loud and distracting and made him feel vulnerable.

Then, his pack. He put it on the end of the burnt-orange couch. Then, stretched out his sleeping bag to keep their dust off him and his dust off them. A really good arrangement all the way around. Then, shoes. He took his off. He would prefer slippers but found some plastic bags and put them over his feet so as not to cause a problem. He'd look for slippers later that might be his size but regardless he wouldn't leave footprints on the nice floor now.

He sat down to watch TV. Which was not, of course, working. Oh, but it was. She must have just left and the company had not yet shut it off. He would watch it then for thirty seconds or thirty minutes or thirty days, whichever it stayed on. Ah, then he could have easy coffee. So he made some. Because there would be voltage to work the water pump for at least as long as the TV played.

He dug through the newspapers he found by the couch and made a tiny dog out of paper coupons. He put it by his couch bed so it could protect him at night, bay at the stars and let him sleep in peace. Tomorrow, he'd look for sugar and salt packets that he could fold and flatten and finesse into beings to keep him company for the long haul of winter.

In the meantime, he laid out on the orange couch, feet stretched out forever. His foot felt something through the plastic. He twitched his toes and found a pipe. An old fashioned kind grannies smoked before grannies didn't smoke anymore. It was brown in the way old things are always brown, especially well loved ones.

A pipe from cob, the mouth end bitten the way it's not supposed to be but is anyway. Little gnaws and big gnaws and medium size gnaws. This, he was jealous of and would have a hard time not stealing. He put it on the end table like a prize, but one he was not yet sure he could accept. He pulled out a bit of his tobacco and filled it. Then, changed his mind and picked up a pencil left behind for doing the crossword and chewed it instead.

***

When Mrs. Sunday had left three days before to go see Tony Bennett, she'd put her teeth in and taken her glasses off. She wanted be able to kiss him but maybe not see him so good.

It turned out in her favor. She couldn't quite make out which direction the old doughboy's blue eyes squinted from her balcony seat. She could tell those feet and those hips were pointed straight for her, though, crooning every song to the top level and a bit to the left.

When he put down his microphone for Fly Me To The Moon and projected his eighty-four year old voice to the way back seats, his eyes locked on hers and he noted the seat number, somehow visible through her peach flowerdy jacket, her brooch, her lungs and the scritch of her neck. She doesn't have a gizzard or he could have seen through that, too. She doesn't take his flirting too seriously, though, and doesn't approach him with the other fans at the stage door. She walks off down the street, headed for her car, and the three hundred miles ahead.

Mrs. Sunday made the trip into the city to see a show once a year. She had to cross not only two county lines but a state one as well. Her fingers got to the edge of the map and then had to fumble in the glove box to pull out the next one. There was something about a long trip that exceeded the confines of her map that always loosened the fear in her chest that built up from daily life.

It was a long drive and she always made a week of it, stopping at rest stops, tasting the world's spices and admiring the lotions and potions of all its worldly people. She had boughten her Tony tickets three months before and had been saving her pennies in the bottom of every grape jelly jar she had for the trip itself.

She had seen The Dollmaker once and also the Rockettes when they were on tour. She had never seen pantyhose like that and wasn't sure they even sold them over where she lived. She had pulled up her socks that trip once she stood up from her seat and had to keep pulling them up the long walk back to the car. Pantyhose weren't as warm, it's true, but they weren't known for scooching down as much, either.

The wind was up and her brooch clankety clanked on her chest, and the hem of her skirt threatened to expose the arthritic knob of her ankles. She was making good time, considering.

A block near, she sat on a porch where no one seemed to live and took in the sights. Same almost-dead tree from last year. Something freshly painted, she could tell by the smell. Not like milk paint at all. She pulled some plantain up out of the yard and plucked the strings out. She tied them into knots and then a tiny ring as she waited for her breath.

When it came, she was off again and this time enjoying the sights more. When she saw the red sign on the fence, she paused. Another car was in her space by the lone tree. There were acorns on its windshield, not hers.

It came to her like a thought from God. She had made a mistake. Her car was at the bus station back home. Her black shoes had walked the concrete of the last thirteen years, forgetting it was the fourteenth. This year, she had been brave, wanting to fraternize with worldly people and their perfumes on a long trip. She had taken the bus.

She had hoped a strange gentleman might offer her a bologna sandwich like in a paper novel. He might have reached over from his seat across the aisle and offered her his handkerchief as well. Or, she might have just watched the young children careening up and down the aisles with no manners. That would have been entertainment, too.

She twisted her ring. Her feet stopped and moved a bit sideways. It was simply not her car. The bus station was seventeen blocks back the other way. Plus two green overpasses. She sat.

When she roused herself, she was stove up from the nap on the step by the fence by the car that was not hers. It was just dusk, as Tony had been a matinee. Tony was always a matinee. The sun was gone, and she had goosebumps. She pulled her keys out of her pocket and flipped them. Jaunty. She picked up her pocketbook and started off, literally, toward the sunset. Twenty minutes later, she'd crossed three and a half streets, but one didn't count as she was window looking.

She pulled her jacket closer as the wind picked up. She stopped at a bright, little storefront with a sun painted on the window. The walls were lemony, and something smelled like tangerine. She went in and got some bread and coffee. When she felt better, she ordered a meal.

In the city, she would eat...she didn't know. She searched for celebration food. Nothing looked good and no menu item had exclamation marks that might show the most festive choices a person might make to ensure their lone day in the city did not end with a sad swallow. She wanted the kind of food you set afire. But what was that?

It seemed to her that the walls couldn't make up their mind on what was plumb. They tipped a bit from side to side, in a woozy sort of way.

But, she settled herself with a Reuben, loving the smell of sauerkraut. The pumpernickel was warm on her thumb and she considered -perhaps- her fingers were a might cold. She looked around for pears on the menu and then on other diners' plates when she found none. She thought a waitress might could pour a little wine on one and it might aflame. That might be okay.

A moth flew out of her coat. But it didn't. Mrs. Sunday closed her pocketbook. She was ready to be home. She was not ready for the clankety clank of her brooch. She put it in her pocketbook. Down deep.

The lemony feeling was gone from the cafeteria. The back of the sun decal was gray and scratchy inside. In the underneath part, someone had written "yes and no". She left a quarter for the waitress and a penny for the fairies and set to walking. Four blocks away she thought a quarter wasn't enough, but the table corner where you left such things by the sugar packets and the false cream was so far back. The strange triangle pattern on the rug by the table leg was just forcing its way into her journey when she smelled manure.

And warm horse. She twisted. There was no horse sound, because there was so much city everywhere. It clappity clapped toward her pulling a buggy. A buggy. She hailed it as you might a cab on the television. It stopped. A man with a stove pipe hat asked her did she want a ride?

"I do. But how much? And, what's his name?"

The stove pipe man, Sam, said, "20 bucks" and "Fred." Also, "Getting chilly out."

"I'm going to the bus station. With the racing dogs."

"I can't take you but around in a circle." But he said it city, so it came out: "No can do, lady."

She blistered, then balmed herself. "Where can I go for 50 cents?"

"For that, you can sit here while I drink my soda."

And she did. She did.

She gave him another quarter, for his shiny eyes, when she got off. He tipped his hat, a most un-city-like thing to do. And, he wasn't joking.

After the horse, she found a bench. Long enough for three people. Her lips were purple. Then more purple. The entire city of sidewalks had already sold its heat to the night. The concrete beneath her own feet and her bench itself followed suit and shoved the cold deep into her bones. She'd had a funny feeling in her gullet all day like something wanted out. It had quieted down a bit when Tony sang to it but now it was back.

Suddenly, Mrs. Sunday's life was like a crab that scuttled up and out from every toe and finger, near and far. Her life was determined but not desperate to get back home. Her entire face went purple, not a good color for a person but she went well with the night. A fine complexion for lying back under the evening sky. The stars raced in their heavens, but slowly. Everything felt the winter coming. The dipper stretched the crick in its neck and went back to pointing true north once the tremor passed. She had lost an inch of curl in her hair but her spine had lengthened and her heels pointed an odd direction.

The next day when the sun rose, Mrs. Sunday did not. She was reclined and a might chilly. There was a plastic, rubbery sheet and some new jewelry on her toe. Not a bangle or a bell but a tag. A man flicked it.

Nicer than you might a fly, but still. "She's homeless. Look at those crusty feet." His mama had not raised him with the edict, *Children only need shoes when they're in school.* He looked at her eyes and her teeth. Her fingernails. She had cleaned them up nice for Tony Bennett. "They're filthy." He was not a gardener, did not dig in the dirt for his potatoes most evenings. He looked in the plastic box at her brooch. "My aunt had one of those."

He sat down and smoked on his ballpoint while he began to type. Inside her veins, Mrs. Sunday's blood sat still. Not taking its morning constitutional. Too chilly out. It settled in her in a new way. Stretched out for the long haul. Moving its toes and wriggling its elbows til it felt just right. A little stiff, but not bad, considering.

The blood was still a little soupy but mostly firming up like a chicken's does before you mix it up for dark and dirty rice. But, hers would set here, not flecked with a fork into rice in a black iron skillet. Useless, true. But, still, it enjoyed the rest. Wouldn't you? Some of the blood was tired and went to her knees and sat there. Not playing poker, exactly, but waiting for something, something grander.

***

The man back at Mrs. Sunday's home, Uncle Son, was folding a piece of paper into a gull. It had no soul, being paper, but was nice looking just the same. You might think he'd have been to the sea, but you'd be wrong. He had heard the water birds on a record and seen them in a filmstrip at the library. They were white, but this one was blue and longer somehow.

In Uncle Son's brown-headed head, the gull had a mournful cry. He went and set it on the table next to his cup of tinny orange juice from the metal can. The electric company was lazy and still hadn't shut off the lady's power. His orange juice was even chilly from the fridge. Imagine.

The TV company, too, was playing fast and easy with her winter turn off days. Her bill would be humongous if they weren't careful. Maybe they were late coming into this area or her disconnect was on a paper that was behind the paper that fell under a chair in a back room. He twisted his fingers for a moment, paused, and hoped it stayed there. He could keep himself from using the electricity at night when it would be noticeable.

The woman must have been in a hurry when she was closing up her home for the winter. She had left chicken in the fridge on a plate with a container of custardy darkness, like the blood his aunt used to cook drained straight from a rooster's neck for Sunday supper. His aunt had mixed it with a bit of flour and made a dark brown gravy with black specks of pepper so nothing, but nothing, was wasted.

He was feeling braver today and headed back to check out the rest of the house. He hoped she had a bit of chaw or tobacco in a tin, on a dresser or next to a bed. He would still use the couch, preferred it even, but the pipe would be a nice reward for keeping her home safe from intruders for the season. He put his plastic-bagged feet on her pink carpet and began to know the lay of the land.

Mrs. Sunday's Apple-Headed Doll

Take an apple, and don't eat it. Let it sit for a bit, and look at it til you start to get an idea of exactly where the person is in it. Then peel it, but don't core it (or do).

Take your knife and cut slits for the eyes, nose and mouth. You can also do a bit of something for the cheeks if you want, but that's a bit advanced, and you may want to wait for your second time around for that.

Then, let it set off to the side somewhere where it can dry nicely. If you are modern and in a hurry, then you can try drying it in a very slow oven, absolutely no higher than two hundred, but I can't promise anything.

Your apple granny will age as she dries, though for all I know, she's an apple grandpa. I've just always heard of them as women. Your first effort will be fun but not perfect. No apple doll ever is. You are working in combination with Mother Nature, remember, and she always has the upper hand.

Next time, if there is a next time, you can try different types of cuts and slits and slices to see what they will do, too. Have fun! If this isn't a project to make you appreciate wrinkles, I don't know what will.

-The End-

A Few Storybooks Meriwether Enjoys...

Gorilla, My Love by Toni Cade Bambara
Had I A Hundred Mouths by William Goyen
Saturday Night at the Pahala Theatre by Lois-Ann
Yamanaka
The Stories of Breece D'J Pancake by Breece D'J Pancake
Sassafrass, Cypress and Indigo, Ntozake Shange
The Lone Ranger and Tonto Fistfight in Heaven by
Sherman Alexie
The Little Disturbances of Man by Grace Paley
Dubliners by James Joyce
The Complete Stories by Flannery O'Connor
Almost anything by J. Frank Dobie, Toni Morrison or Zora
Neale Hurston
The House on Mango Street by Sandra Cisneros
Aesop's Fables
Bastard Out of Carolina by Dorothy Allison
Tales Of The City series by Armistead Maupin
To Build A Fire by Jack London, and, of course,
the *Foxfire* books, which are true to life and so have all the
story you could ever want in them.

Book Club Questions

Meriwether loves book clubs. She'd be happy to talk with yours by phone or Skype. Contact: moconnor50@hotmail.com

- Would you taste any of the recipes from this book? Do you think they're meant to be eaten or just included for humor or as cultural touchstones?

- Can a book with some type of death in almost every story still be life affirming?

- Are these stories violent? Are they offensive?

- Is Gardenia a cruel person? What about Matilda? Mr. Johnston? How do you define what cruelty is? Does it change according to the situation?

- Why were the Marvels of Peru trying to get back home? That species of flowers literally do break two of Mendel's scientific rules. What in your life goes against the rules but instead of annoying you, somehow inspires you? Is there anything you're always trying to get back home to?

- Was Malachi wrong? Was his father? Does intent matter? What do you think happened the next day?

- Why did the father in *The Mail Comes Twice* draw the apartment rabbits?

- In *Second Cousin*, a man puts shoe polish on the corpse of his famous cousin. Was this disrespectful? What makes something respectful or disrespectful?

- What unique foods, habits, toys or sayings might show up if you were to write something based in your family's culture? Would most people be surprised by this side of you? Is it something you feel comfortable sharing with others, or something you keep behind closed doors?

- What does your family eat that might be considered a "real life recipe"?

- Overall, did you find this book filled with savagery or grace? Humor or pain? Something completely different?

- Do you feel any differently about either life or death after reading this book?

www.ingramcontent.com/pod-product-compliance
Lightning Source LLC
Chambersburg PA
CBHW020316150626
46552CB00022B/2898